About the Book

"An otter ought to be honest," Papa Otter tells Andrew. "It's the family motto." Eager to please, Andrew puts Papa's instructions into practice the very next day. But instead of getting the praise he expects for his honesty, he soon learns that he has embarrassed Mama, angered the neighbors, and disappointed Papa. After another talk, Andrew tries again, with unexpected results, proving that one can understand the words without getting the idea.

A LET ME READ BOOK

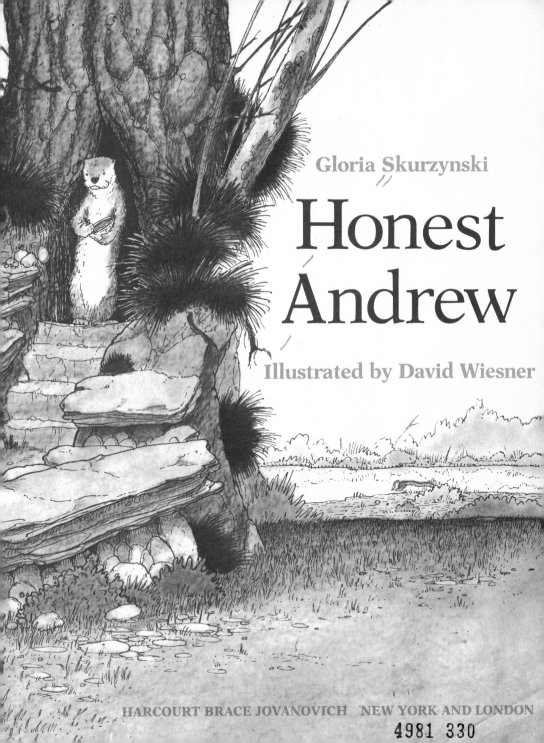

Gloria Skurzynski

Honest Andrew

Illustrated by David Wiesner

HARCOURT BRACE JOVANOVICH   NEW YORK·AND·LONDON

For Kristin Ann

Text copyright © 1980 by Gloria Skurzynski
Illustrations copyright © 1980 by David Wiesner

All rights reserved. No part of
this publication may be reproduced or
transmitted in any form or by any means,
electronic or mechanical, including photocopy,
recording, or any information storage and
retrieval system, without permission
in writing from the publisher.

Requests for permission to make copies of
any part of the work should be mailed to:
Permissions, Harcourt Brace Jovanovich, Inc.,
757 Third Avenue, New York, New York 10017

Printed in the United States of America

Set in VIP Aster

First edition
B C D E

Andrew Otter sat down at the table with his mama and his papa, inside the family den. "What's for dinner?" he asked. "I'm starved."

"Tonight we're having crayfish," his mama told him. "Eat everything on your plate, so you'll grow up to be a big, strong otter like Papa."

Andrew moaned to himself. He hated crayfish! But he didn't want to hurt his mama's feelings. He knew how hard she'd worked over her special dish.

"This is really good," Andrew's papa said, crunching the crayfish. "Isn't this good, Andrew?"

"Uh huh." Andrew chewed hard and tried to swallow. He really tried, but his throat wouldn't open up.

"I'll have a second helping," Papa Otter said. "Here, have some more, Andrew." He piled more crayfish on Andrew's plate.

Andrew kept chewing, but the food just wouldn't go down. Instead, it pushed itself into his cheeks. He took more bites and chewed again, not swallowing any of it. More and more food got squished inside his cheeks until they puffed up like two balloons.

"Now you may have dessert," Mama Otter said, placing a dish of strawberry ice in front of Andrew.

Andrew loved strawberry ice! But how could he eat dessert when his mouth was full of crayfish? "Excuse me," he mumbled. "I have to go outside."

"Why?" his papa asked.

His mama also asked, "Why?"

"Because I want to . . . to smell the sweet petunias," Andrew tried to say. But his mouth was so full that the words sounded like "fmell the fweep PATOO-IES!" On the last word he nearly blew out both cheekfuls of mashed-up crayfish.

Andrew hurried through the long tunnel that opened onto the riverbank. When he reached the bank, he took a deep breath. Then he spit his food far out into the water.

"Ahem!"

Andrew turned to see his papa standing behind him.

"What do you think you're doing?" his papa asked.

"Uh, I was just baiting the fish traps," Andrew stammered.

"You're not telling the truth, Andrew. I followed you. You had your whole dinner in your mouth, and you spit it into the river. Why did you do that?"

"Because I *hate crayfish!*" Andrew cried.

"Why didn't you say so?"

"I didn't want to hurt Mama's feelings. And you would have made me eat it anyway. Wouldn't you?"

"I suppose so," Papa Otter said, "but I wouldn't have given you more. What you did wasn't honest, Andrew. And then you lied about it. Come with me." He took Andrew by the ear. "You and I are going to have a talk about honesty."

Papa Otter marched Andrew back down the tunnel and into his study. "Andrew, do you see that sign on the wall?" he asked. "Can you read the words?"

"Not all of them," Andrew answered.

"It says, AN OTTER OUGHT TO BE HONEST. That's been the otter motto for as long as anyone can remember. We otters are famous for being honest and truthful. Why, once upon a time, an otter walked four miles just to return a fish that another otter had dropped beside a stream. And then there was a young otter, not much older than you, who dug a big hole in his father's favorite mud slide. The slide was quite spoiled."

"What happened to the little otter?" Andrew wondered.

"When his father asked, 'Who spoiled my slide?' the otter cub stood right up and said, 'I did it, Father. I cannot tell a lie.'"

"Did he get a spanking?"

"No, he didn't," Andrew's papa replied. "His father was so proud of the cub for speaking the truth that he didn't punish him. You see, Andrew, we otters value honesty above all else. If you want to make Papa proud, you must be honest and truthful."

"I will, Papa," Andrew promised. "From now on I'll always tell the truth."

"Good boy!" Andrew's papa smiled so that his mustache turned up.

The next day, while Andrew was sitting on the riverbank thinking about honesty, his mother called to him. "Do you want to go to the store with me?" she asked.

It was easy to be truthful about that.

"Yes, I'd like to go," he replied.

In a little while Andrew and Mama Otter were walking along the forest path. It was a lovely day, and a lot of other creatures strolled through the forest. Coming toward them on the path was a

stooped, squinty-eyed animal wearing glasses.

"That's Professor Newton Beaver," Andrew's mama told him. "He's a well-known scholar. Be polite to him, Andrew."

"Yes, Mama."

"How do you do, Professor Beaver," Mama Otter said.

"How do you do, madam." The professor nodded. "And is this your little son? How are you, young man?"

Andrew thought hard. He remembered his promise to be honest. "Well," he began, "I have this cut on my back paw. I got it last week when I was playing tag on the riverbank. A thorn scratched me. And my nose hurts . . . see right there? An eel bit me while I was swimming in the river. I think it was last Thursday, but it might have been Wednesday. . . . No, it was probably Thursday. I'm pretty sure. Then last night I felt bad because my papa got mad at me. The reason why he got mad was that we were having crayfish for dinner, and I . . ."

The smile on Professor Beaver's face had grown stiff. His eyes looked funny. They seemed to be moving away from each other. "Fine boy, fine boy," he muttered, patting Andrew on the head and hurrying off down the path.

"*Andrew, why did you talk so much?*" his mama asked.

"He asked me how I was, and I wanted to tell him the truth."

Mama Otter sighed. "Look, Aunt Prissy Porcupine is coming toward us. She's very fussy about manners. If she asks how you are, don't go on and on. Just say, 'Fine, thank you.'"

"But, Mama . . ."

"*Andrew!*" She gave him a warning look, then smiled to greet Aunt Prissy Porcupine. "Hello, Aunt Prissy. I haven't seen you in a long, long time."

"My dear!" Aunt Prissy held her cheek forward to be kissed. "And this is Andrew. I do declare, I can't believe how much he's grown. Why, you're quite a big otter, Andrew."

"That's not the truth. I am *not* a big otter," Andrew said loudly. "I don't go up any higher than my mama's front paws."

"Oooooh!" Aunt Prissy bristled until her quills stuck out in angry points. "Did you hear what that cub said to me? Why, in my day, if a little tyke sassed his elders like that . . ."

Andrew's mama pulled his paw so hard that his arm hurt. "Excuse us, Aunt Prissy," she said through her teeth. "We're in a bit of a hurry."

Andrew wondered why his mama was glaring so angrily at him.

Before she had a chance to tell him, Mrs. Hazel Woodchuck came into sight, pushing a baby buggy. "Yoo hoo, Mrs. Otter," Mrs. Woodchuck called out. "I want you to meet the newest child in my family. This is my daughter, Piney Sue."

Andrew watched the strange changes in his mama's face. Her scowl smoothed out to make room for a polite smile. "What a beautiful baby!" Andrew's mama said, chucking the little woodchuck under the chin. "Isn't she darling?"

Andrew stood on tiptoe to see inside the buggy. "Darling? She's ugly," he said. "Her face is all wrinkled. She looks like she slid facedown on a mud slide."

"*Andrew!*" His mama yanked his paw so hard that his feet flew off the ground. She turned him toward home, pulling him so fast that when his feet did touch the ground, he had to run to keep up.

"I've never been so embarrassed!" Mama Otter shouted. "Just wait till I get you home, young man!"

"I was only being honest, Mama! That baby isn't pretty at all."

"Not another word out of you! When your papa hears about this, I don't know what he'll do to you."

Andrew wanted to tell her that he'd only been speaking honestly and truthfully, just as he had promised. He wanted to ask if they couldn't please go on to the store, where he'd hoped to get a strawberry ice. But the look on his mama's face told him he'd better keep quiet.

He spent the rest of the day sitting on a chair facing the wall. When his papa came home, Andrew could hear his mama telling Papa Otter about all the things he'd said to Professor Beaver, to Aunt Prissy Porcupine, and to Mrs. Woodchuck.

Andrew's papa cleared his throat a couple of times, quite loudly, then called Andrew to him. "Why were you so rude today?" he asked.

"I was just trying to make you proud of me," Andrew explained.

"Proud of you! You bored Professor Beaver. You insulted Aunt Prissy. You hurt Mrs. Woodchuck. Don't you know it's wrong to say unkind things?"

"Then I shouldn't be honest and truthful?" Andrew asked.

"Of course you should. But you mustn't hurt people's feelings."

"Last night I was trying not to hurt Mama's feelings when I really hated crayfish," Andrew said. "You got mad at me then because I didn't tell the truth." His voice choked with tears.

"That was dif . . ." his papa sputtered.
"That was . . . um . . . humph. . . . That
was. . . . Oh, my!" Papa Otter's shoulders
drooped. His mustache drooped. He
looked so bewildered that Andrew felt
sorry for him.

Andrew was silent for a moment. Then
he touched his papa's shoulder. "Papa,"
he said, "is this what I should do? Should
I always tell the truth, but be as nice and
polite about it as I can?"

"Yes! That's it! That's *exactly* what you should do." Andrew's papa sighed a big sigh of relief. He smiled so widely that his mustache curled. "Well, Andrew, I'm glad we got that straightened out," he said. "Now let's find out what's for dinner. I'm starved."

"Tonight we're having salamander stew," Mama Otter called out.

Andrew slumped down on his chair. "Mama," he said, "you are the sweetest, nicest mama in the whole world. Your eyes are big and bright. Your fur is warm and soft. You wear pretty earrings, and *I HATE SALAMANDER STEW!*"

Gloria Skurzynski was born near Pittsburgh, Pennsylvania, and attended Mount Mercy College. She did not begin to write until many years later, after the youngest of her five daughters, the inspiration for *Honest Andrew*, started school. Ms. Skurzynski has written several well-received books, including *Two Fools and a Faker: Three Lebanese Folktales, In a Bottle with a Cork on Top*, and *The Poltergeist of Jason Morey*.

David Wiesner was born in Plainfield, New Jersey, and then moved with his family to Bound Brook, New Jersey, where he grew up. Mr. Wiesner is a graduate of the Rhode Island School of Design. *Honest Andrew* is the first book he has illustrated.